Cosmo is a dodo. He is one of a unique species of bird that once lived on our planet. Hundreds of years ago, he and the other dodos lived peacefully on the island of Mauritius, isolated from man and their charted land.

Approximately 300 years ago, and only a few years after the first sailors arrived on the island, the dodos had almost completely disappeared. Only Cosmo remained. He was the last dodo.

With his new friend, 3R-V the spaceship, Cosmo now travels from planet to planet in search of other dodos like him. Together Cosmo and 3R-V have great adventures.

D1310426

Les Aventures de Cosmo le dodo de l'espace: L'étrange substance names, characters and related indicia are trademarks of Racine et Associés Inc. All Rights Reserved.

Originally published as *Les Aventures de Cosmo le dodo de l'espace: L'étrange substance* by Origo Publications, POB 4 Chambly, Quebec J3L 4B1, 2008

English translation © 2011 by Tundra Books
This English edition published in Canada by Tundra Books, 2011
75 Sherbourne Street, Toronto, Ontario M5A 2P9

Published in the United States by
Tundra Books ofNorthern New York,
P.O. Box 1030, Plattsburgh, New York 12901

Library of Congress Control Number: 2010928799

Library and Archives Canada Cataloguing in Publication

Pat Rac, 1963-
[Étrange substance. English]
The mysterious substance / Patrice Racine.

(The adventures of Cosmo the dodo bird)
Translation of: L'étrange substance.
For ages 6-9.
ISBN 978-1-77049-247-9

I. Title. II. Title: Étrange substance. English. III. Series:
Pat Rac, 1963- .Adventures of Cosmo the dodo bird.

PS8631.A8294E8713 2011   jC843'.6   C2010-903169-5

We acknowledge the financial support of the Government of Canada through the Book Publishing Industry Development Program (BPIDP) and that of the Government of Ontario through the Ontario Media Development Corporation's Ontario Book Initiative. We further acknowledge the support of the Canada Council for the Arts and the Ontario Arts Council for our publishing program.

ONTARIO ARTS COUNCIL
CONSEIL DES ARTS DE L'ONTARIO

For more information on the international rights, please visit www.cosmothedodobird.com

Printed in Mexico

1 2 3 4 5 6   16 15 14 13 12 11

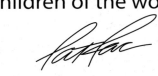

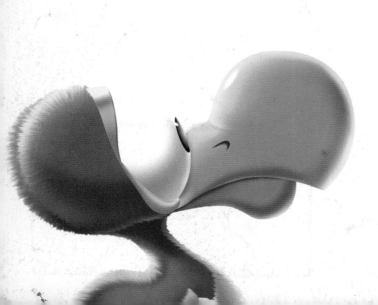

For all the children of the world

THE ADVENTURES OF
COSMO
THE DODO BIRD™

THE MYSTERIOUS SUBSTANCE

Tundra Books

After searching the universe without finding any trace of a single dodo bird, 3R-V and Cosmo spot a planet that looks just like Earth. They land in a luscious green field and immediately set out to explore it.
Soon they find footsteps in the soft grass.

"We may finally be on the right track, 3R-V. Let's follow these footprints. Maybe they'll lead us to dodos at last." Cosmo is very excited.

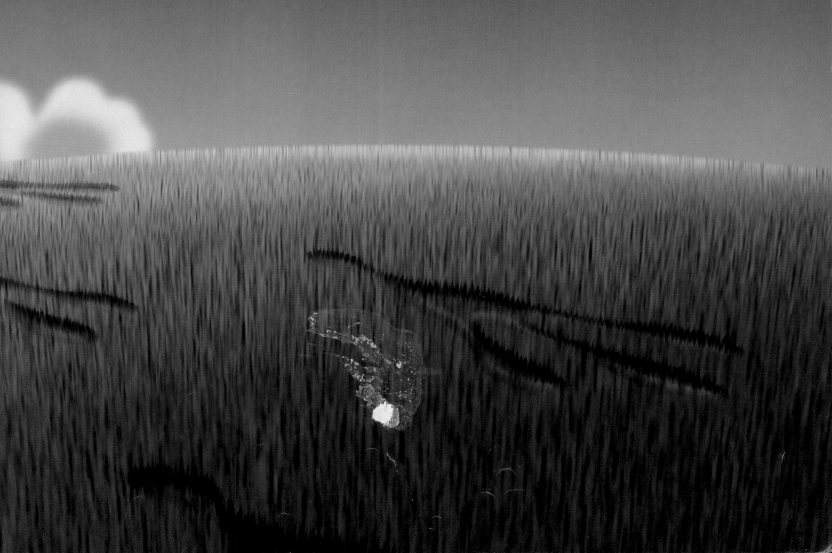

"Slow down, Cosmo!" 3R-V tries to keep pace with his friend, but he's getting tired. "I can't keep up!"

"You can do it. Look, there are more tracks here." Cosmo follows the tracks so intently that he almost bumps into the creature that has made them.

"Oh! You're not a dodo!" says Cosmo. He holds back his tears.

"I'm Fabrico the Workman. Who – what are you?"

"I'm Cosmo the Dodo Bird, and this is 3R-V. He's a spaceship."

3R-V is staring at Fabrico's big glass flask full of yucky, green gunk.
"What *is* that stuff, Fabrico?" 3R-V is curious and alarmed.

"This? It's nothing to worry about. It's just leftovers from the factory where I work. If you'll just give me a hand, I can finish my job." Fabrico leans against the flask.

"You're not planning to dump this weird gunk into the river, are you?" asks Cosmo.

"You bet I am! Those are my orders."

"But think what it will do to this clean, shining river!" 3R-V is upset. "You'll pollute it!"

"What are you? Some kind of expert?"

"You don't have to be an expert to know this is wrong," says Cosmo. "Just think before you cause a disaster!"

"I don't get paid to think! Anyway, what harm could this little bit of waste possibly do to so much water?"

"Well, *you* sure don't know!" says 3R-V.

"I'm *positive* that it's okay." But Fabrico doesn't sound quite as sure, now.

"Would you be willing to taste it? Would you drink some?" asks Cosmo.

Fabrico stammers an excuse. "Uh, well, no, but it's just because I'm not thirsty."

"Aha! You know you can't drink this stuff.
So you must also know it's harmful to the environment," says Cosmo.

Fabrico glares at him. "Leave me alone! I need a little time!"

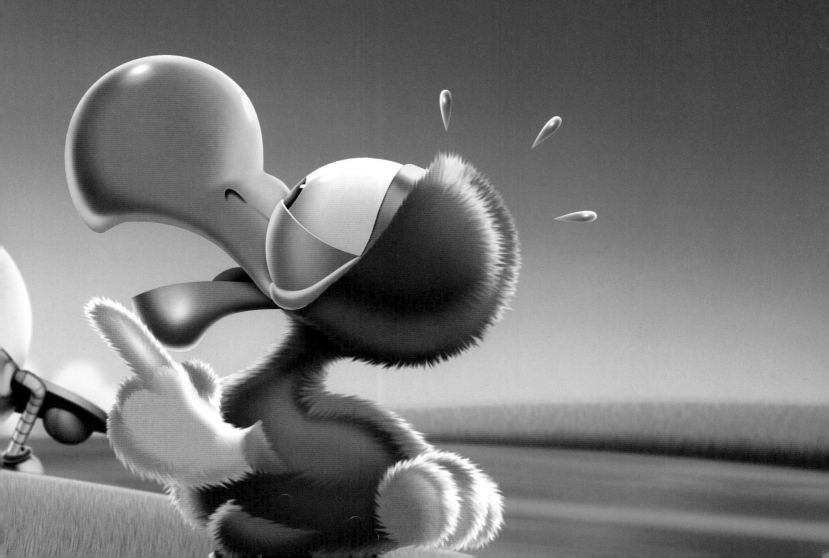

Cosmo and 3R-V decide to give Fabrico a few minutes to think about what they've said.

As they walk away, Fabrico captures a harmless lizard.

He puts a drop or two of the strange liquid on the little creature's tongue.

"Cosmo! 3R-V! Come back!" Fabrico calls.
"See? There was nothing to worry about. The lizard tasted it
 and nothing happened.

"What have you done? Poor little lizard!" Cosmo is very angry.

"Don't be such a worrywart! She's fine. The goo is harmless, just like I thought."

"Look!" cries 3R-V.

The lizard's sharp, tiny teeth have grown into fangs. Her skin is slimy.
And she's huge!

She lets out an angry roar.

Cosmo and 3R-V take off.
Fabrico is left to fend for himself.

"I sure hope he can run fast," says Cosmo.

Fabrico is trying hard, but he can't outrun the monster he has created.

Just when he is too tired to take another step, Fabrico is faced with another terrible danger. He has come to the edge of a pit.

Down,
   down,
      down, he falls, into the dark hole.

"We have to help him, 3R-V," says Cosmo, but the little spaceship is already diving full speed into the pit. With a metal foot, 3R-V grabs the terrified workman.

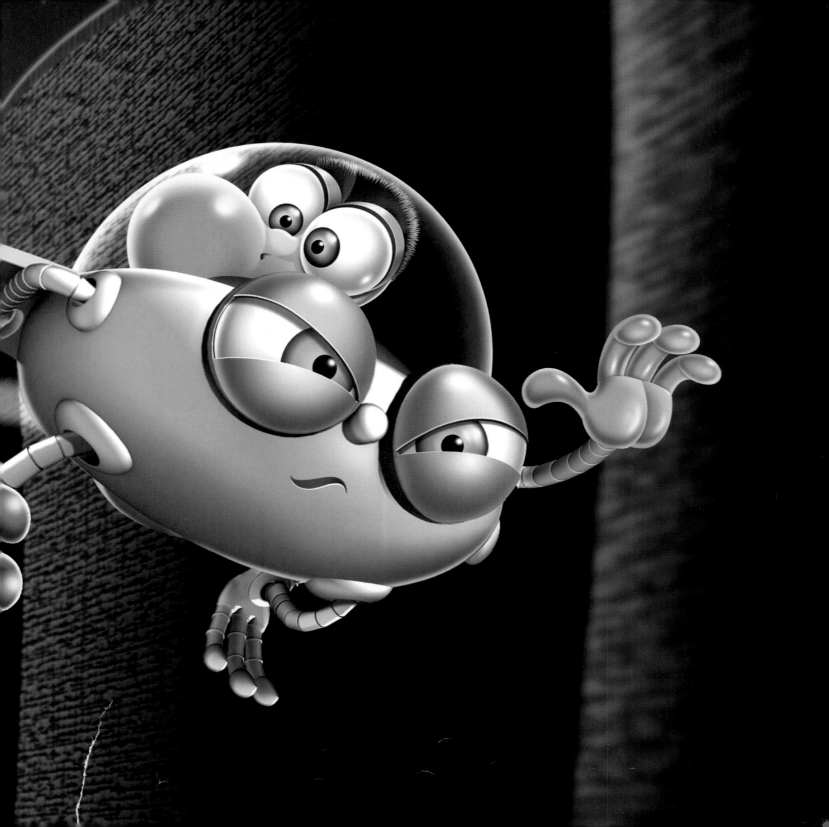

Meanwhile, the lizard seems to be recovering.

3R-V places Fabrico safely back on the green grass.

"Whew! That was close. Without you, I would have been lost.
And look! Thank goodness. The Lizard is back to normal!"

But if only a few drops changed her into a monster, can you imagine what would have happened if you had poured the whole flask into the river?" says Cosmo.

Fabrico shakes his head. "It would have been a terrible disaster. I have to tell the others how important it is to protect nature so that we never make that mistake."

After promising to keep in touch, Cosmo and 3R-V continue on their mission.

"I think Fabrico's learned that you can't abuse nature," says 3R-V.

"Right. And I'm sure he'll tell the others how important it is to work together to protect the environment," says Cosmo. "After all, Nature always treats us the same way we treat it."

3R-V is a kind and gentle robot-ship invented by a scientist
on the planet Earth. This scientist cared a great deal about nature
and the environment. He built the robot-ship according to the following
principles: reduce, re-use, and recycle. He named the ship 3R-V and gave
it a propulsion system that uses a renewable, non-polluting source of energy.
3R-V is also equipped with incredible technological resources.

3R-V is Cosmo's best friend, and, together, they travel from planet to planet
in search of other dodos.